ARMADILLO

MARY ELISE MONSELL

Illustrations by SYLVIE WICKSTROM

ATHENEUM   1991   NEW YORK

Collier Macmillan Canada   *Toronto*
Maxwell Macmillan International Publishing Group
New York   Oxford   Singapore   Sydney

Library of Congress Cataloging-in-Publication Data Monsell, Mary Elise.
  Armadillo / by Mary Elise Monsell; illustrated by Sylvie Wickstrom. p.   cm.
  Summary: The other animals are concerned when Armadillo disappears into his house every time it rains, until they discover just how dry and cozy he is there. ISBN 0-689-31676-3 [1. Armadillos—Fiction. 2. Animals—Fiction.]
I. Wickstrom, Sylvie, ill. II. Title PZ7.M7626Ar 1991 [E]—dc20 90-19135

To Vicki,
who helped me find peace
in the worst of storms.
This armadillo sincerely thanks you
—MEM

To David, my armadillo brother
—SW

Sometimes it rains where Armadillo lives.
Sometimes it doesn't. When it sometimes rains,
Armadillo crawls deep into his dark, dark burrow.
He finds the right spot. He lights one candle. He
reads one book. Then he falls asleep.

No one really *knew* that about Armadillo in Oklahoma when it rained.

Everyone knew he was all right when it wasn't raining. The prairie dogs had seen him once roasting pecans in the afternoon sun.

They said it was Armadillo who left warm
pecans outside all of the mouse and rabbit and
prairie dog houses. They knew Armadillo left
other fine things too: Wildflowers. Round stones.
Snail shells.

"What a wonderful day it is," one of the rabbits
said, "to have something from Armadillo left by
your door."

Everyone liked Armadillo. They just didn't see
him very much.

And when it rained, no one *ever* saw Armadillo, and that was when the animals began to worry.

"How can anyone be alone in the rain and be all right?" they said.

"He's very quiet," they said.

"How can anyone be that quiet?" they asked.

"He must be sad," they decided.

So when it rained, the mice and the prairie dogs and the gray rabbits opened umbrellas and walked in the rain to Armadillo's house. They didn't want Armadillo to be alone.

The prairie dogs built cooking fires. They made soup and baked corn bread in the coals and cracked pecans into baskets. All the while the rain went *ping-ping-ping* on their open umbrellas.

"Someone should knock on Armadillo's door," said a mouse.

"What if he doesn't like loud knocking?" asked another mouse.

"We should just stay here," said the rabbit.

"In case he needs something to eat," said a prairie dog.

"I wonder if Armadillo is flooding?" said a mouse.

So the mice hammered bridges over puddles.
The iron pots blackened. And the rabbits talked
very loudly about how long it had been raining
and just how wet everything was.

But Armadillo was not one bit bothered about
the rain. Armadillo was asleep beside his one
candle in just the right spot in Oklahoma.

Until it stopped raining.

"He can't be sad about the rain if it's not raining," said a prairie dog.

Then all of the mice and the prairie dogs and the gray rabbits shook out their umbrellas and their soggy fur. They doused their cooking fires with rainwater. And since they were very tired, they went to their own houses to go to sleep.

When Armadillo woke up from his very nice nap he was always hungry. He was ready for an after-rain, Armadillo breakfast. He looked around outside his house and wondered why there were baskets of corn bread and cracked pecans and bowls of soup left next to water-soaked cooking fires.

Armadillo thought it was very nice that someone had left him an after-rain breakfast. But it was very strange, he thought, that he never saw anyone when it wasn't raining…

Until one time when it rained very hard.
Armadillo crawled deep into his dark burrow and
he started to read one very long book. It was such
a good long book that Armadillo was awake when
the other animals came clunking and clanking to
his door.

Outside, the animals were stomping about and
humming in the rain. Puddles had flooded the
tiny mouse bridges. The pecans were soggy and
the fires had gone right out. The animals were
starting to feel cold.

"Armadillo *must* be flooded," they said.

But inside his dry house, Armadillo was putting
on his warm bathrobe, a raincoat, a rain hat, and
rain shoes.

Armadillo was shaking the dust from a very
large umbrella and was crawling to the door of
his burrow.

Outside, over the roar of the thunder, a gray rabbit shouted: "I think we should see if Armadillo is getting wet."

Everyone agreed. But just as they were about to knock, Armadillo threw open his door.

The animals stopped talking and humming and hammering and clanking. And stared.

"Are you all right?" asked Armadillo.

No one answered.

Armadillo asked again. "Are you all right out there?"

The animals stared back at Armadillo.

At last, a prairie dog was able to say: "We were wondering if *you* were all right *in there*. We never see you when it rains. Does the rain make you sad?"

"No," said Armadillo as he looked out at the collected soggy animals. "The rain makes me wet."

"Then you're *really* all right in there?" asked a mouse.

"Oh yes," said Armadillo. "Would you like to come inside and see?"

The rabbits looked at the prairie dogs and the mice looked at the rabbits. Finally, all together they said:

"Yes."

So that was when the mice and the prairie dogs and the rabbits saw that it was very dry inside Armadillo's house. Armadillo showed them his library. He showed them where he kept his candles. He showed them warm dry spots where *they* could all rest while the rain rained outside Armadillo's house.

That was how all the animals found out
Armadillo was all right when it rained. And that
was how Armadillo stopped the animals from
getting wet. Now when it sometimes rains in
Oklahoma, sometimes the animals don't want to
be alone. So the prairie dogs and the mice and the
gray rabbits all go to Armadillo's house, where
they know they can always find just the right spot
to light one candle, read one book, and talk to
Armadillo…

...until he falls asleep.